Chewoo in Nu

Written by Sylvia M. Medina
Art by Joy Eagle, Contributor - Sherri Arnone-Wheat
Published by Green Kids Club, Inc. PO Box 50030 Idaho Falls, ID 83405
Copyright© December 2017 Green Kids Club, Inc. - ALL RIGHTS RESERVED

You can see YooHoo and Friends at www.yoohoofriends.com
Chewoo and YooHoo characters appear in the book with permission of
©Aurora World Corp., www.auroraworld.com

green kids club®

YooHoo® & FRIENDS
©Aurora

Chewoo, a bouncy red squirrel, hears a loud noise outside of her treetop home. She scampers to see what the noise is. Sniff, sniff. What is that smell?

A huge machine burping black smoke is coming straight toward her home and it looks like it's going to chop down her tree!

3

"Oh, no! What am I going to do? I need to get help!" cries Chewoo.

She jumps up and dashes down the tree trunk,

across the clearing to a nearby stand of trees.

Panting, she peeks around the tree and notices that Coops is driving the big stinky machine. The Big Boss must be at it again! This time, he's chopping down trees in the forest.

"Oh no, oh no!" she frets but she scurries from tree to tree trying to stay hidden while looking for her friends.

6

Chewoo worries, "How will I eat this winter
if Coops chops down my tree?"

So Chewoo stops along the way picking up nuts
shoving every one into her cheeks.

Pretty soon her mouth is jam packed and she can barely walk.
"Oh no!" she mumbles.

Soon she is lying on the path with her mouth so full she can't move. She thinks to herself, "What am I going to do now?"

Suddenly she looks up and sees a little boy

walking towards her – and with him is YooHoo.

The Little Boy says – "YooHoo isn't that your friend Chewoo? "

Chewoo is not afraid of the little boy whose name is Tiago
for she has met him before.

YooHoo says, "yes I think it's Chewoo,
but I can't tell because her face is so FAT! Hee hee."

Chewoo can't say a word because her mouth is too full.

She tries to mumble a warning, but it's no use.

Chewoo then tries to spit out a nut - but she can't -
oh my gosh - it's stuck! Tiago goes over with YooHoo
and they try and squeeze her cheeks - nothing will come out!

15

"Oh no what can we do?" YooHoo asks.

Tiago grabs Chewoo by the arm and says, "We need to get back to your home and get your Squirrel Nut Pliers!"

"What, is a Squirrel Nut Plier?" asks YooHoo.

"It's a tool squirrels use when they stuff their cheeks too full," informs Tiago as Chewoo's eyes get bigger and bigger.

Chewoo points at her treehouse and her eyes well up
for she thinks her house is going to be destroyed
by the bad crocodile and his stinky machine.

Tiago picks Chewoo up and vows, "We'll stop him!"
They all start running back toward Chewoo's home. When suddenly
"WHAM!" Tiago trips and falls down, hitting the ground hard.

Chewoo flies from Tiago's arms and

"BAM!" she slams into the ground - causing a nut to shoot

out of her cheeks and hit the crocodile in the eye.

"I want my Mommy!! Wah, wah!" Coops cries.
The bad crocodile yells "Ouch!" then runs off
and leaves Chewoo's home alone!

Without Coops there to hold his machine together,

it quickly falls apart.

With a final "burp" the unused engine becomes trash.

Chewoo, Tiago and YooHoo get busy cleaning up
and recycling Coops' mess - again!

"Hurray!" they all celebrate when they are done.

Chewoo takes the nuts out of her cheeks

and stacks them next to her treehouse.

Chewoo is set for the winter!

© CanStockPhoto/brm1949

Red squirrels live for about 5 years.

They eat pine nuts, acorns, berries, and bark.

They like to live inside trees, but sometimes they will make a nest on a branch next to the tree trunk.

Red Squirrels are endangered because their homes are being destroyed by humans and taken over by Eastern Grey Squirrels.

Did you know that trees make your life better?

Trees absorb carbon dioxide and
harmful gasses from the air
and release oxygen.
This helps to reduce global warming.

What can you do to help trees?

You can ask your parents and teachers to
plant trees in your yard or school grounds.

Make sure to water them every
day until they get stronger.

You can volunteer in your town's
garden projects by weeding and
planting flowers and trees in city gardens.

9 781939 871572